The Hare and the Tortoise

Written and illustrated by Melanie Williamson

Hare said to Tortoise, "I'm so much bigger and better than you."

Tortoise said, "Bigger doesn't always mean better."

3

They both said, "Let's have a race."

4

Hare thought he was so much better than Tortoise that he gave him a head start.

Hare ran past Tortoise.

Slow coach!

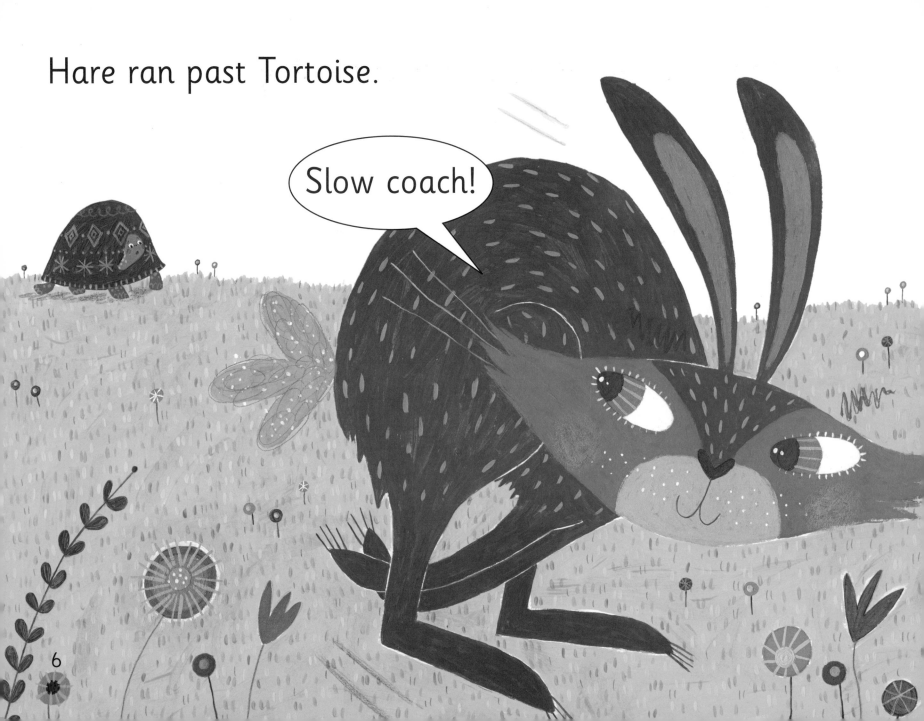

Hare had time to eat. Hare had time to play.

Hare had time to snooze . . .
He fell asleep among the cabbages.
Tortoise slowly plodded past.

8

When Hare woke up, Tortoise had almost won!

FINISH

11

Hare hopped fast, but he couldn't catch up.

Everyone cheered as Tortoise won.

Slow and steady wins the race!

The race

start

finish

14

FINISH

15

Ideas for reading

Written by Clare Dowdall, PhD
Lecturer and Primary Literacy Consultant

Learning objectives: recognise automatically an increasing number of familiar high frequency words; apply phonic knowledge and skills as the prime approach to reading unfamiliar words that are not completely decodable; identify the main events and characters in stories, and find specific information in simple texts; use syntax and context when reading for meaning; retell stories, ordering events using story language; explore familiar themes and characters through improvisation and role-play

Curriculum links: Citizenship

High frequency words: the, and, he, was, but, what, when, they, said, to, so, you, have

Interest words: hare, tortoise, race, bigger, better, head start, slow coach, snooze, cabbages, plodded, slow, steady

Resources: interest word flashcards, black paper, lolly sticks

Word count: 100

Getting started

- Explain that this story is a very famous tale about a race between a hare and a tortoise. Ask if anyone has heard the story before and to discuss it with the group.

- Read the title and the blurb together. Use your finger to point to each word, and model reading longer words, e.g. *bigger, better, happened*. Remind children of the familiar *er* and *ed* endings.

- Ask children to suggest why Hare thinks he is bigger and better than Tortoise. Ask children to suggest what will happen when they have the race, who will win and to give reasons for their answers.

Reading and responding

- Turn to pp2–3. Ask children to read the text aloud with a partner. Discuss how speech is used to tell the story, and show children how speech marks show that a character is speaking. Ask for a pair of children to read the speech with expression, as you narrate.

- Turn to pp4–5 and read the text together. Model how to use the picture to help make meaning from the text and check that children understand what a *head start* is. Discuss whether Hare and Tortoise are friends.

- Ask children to continue reading the story aloud to p13. Support them to use expressive voices and to read more complex words using phonics and contextual clues along with knowledge of familiar word endings.